The Bells of
SANTA LUCIA

Gus Cazzola

with pictures by Pierr Morgan

Philomel Books • New York

Text copyright © 1991 by Gus Cazzola.
Illustration copyright © 1991 by Pierr Morgan.
Published by Philomel Books, a division of The Putnam & Grosset Book Group,
200 Madison Avenue, New York, NY 10016. Published simultaneously in Canada.
All rights reserved. Printed in Hong Kong by South China Printing Co. (1988) Ltd.
Book design by Gunta Alexander.
Library of Congress Cataloging-in-Publication Data
Cazzola, Gus, 1934–   The bells of Santa Lucia/by Gus Cazzola;
illustrated by Pierr Morgan.   p.   cm.
Summary: After her grandmother dies, a little Tuscan girl cannot stand the sound
of bells until the good-hearted schoolmaster introduces her to some belled lambs.
ISBN 0-399-21804-1
[1. Bells-Fiction. 2. Death—Fiction. 3. Tuscany (Italy)—Fiction.] I. Morgan, Pierr, ill.
II. Title. PZ7.C299Be 1991 [E]—dc20 90-19789 CIP AC First impression

To my three kids
Camille, Nadine and Michael—G.C.

To the spirit of Giorgio Morandi, Italian painter (1890–1964)
To Richard, *ti abbraccio*—P.M.

In the sleepy village of Santa Lucia,
where the grapes sip the sun and the sheep
munch the hillside grass, lives Lucinda,
who loves bells.

But Lucinda's granny, Nonna Rosa, rings
a hand bell from her sickbed.
She rings it for her soup.
She rings it for her tea.
She rings it for her prayer beads.
She is ringing it for…

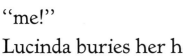"me!"
Lucinda buries her head under the covers.
There…so soft and snug, she smells
the stable straw and Mamma's muslin.
But Lucinda loves Nonna Rosa,
and when the day comes
when the bell rings no more,
Lucinda cries.

Now Santa Lucia is a village of bells.
Its hills ring with bells; its valley dances
to the songs of bells.
Goat bells, dog bells, cat bells, and even
mouse bells.
A big Grandmother Bell bongs from
the village square.
Cow bells tinkle and sheep bells laugh.
And Professore Venuti rings happy bells
in the School of Santa Lucia.
But after Nonna Rosa dies, Lucinda hates all bells.
Each time a bell rings, she covers her head.

Now Santa Lucia is a village of bells.
There is no place to hide from them,
except…inside.
For days Lucinda stays at home.
Mamma must send her friends away
to play without her.
"Lucinda is not feeling well," she moans,
and closes the black curtains to keep out the sun.
"How long will you hide inside?" asks Mamma.
But Lucinda does not speak.
Each year all of the villagers march
in the Festival of the Bells—down winding streets,
past smiling stalls, along sun-kissed walls—
but now they stop beneath Lucinda's window.
"Poor girl," they whisper, "so young to hide…
not to sing with the bells."
Soon Professore Venuti hears of this.

"Afraid of bells? In Santa Lucia?
Ho…ho!" He beams, and crinkles his nose.
"Soon Lucinda will play in the sun again."
With his laugh, with his smile,
Professore Venuti coaxes Lucinda to leave her home.

Gently he leads her to the stalls
behind the school.
Inside stand three lambs—two quite large
and one just a tiny ball of white wool.
Each wears bells around its neck.

One wears three bells. One wears two bells.
And the tiny, tiny lamb wears one bell.
"Bells speak to us," Professore Venuti says.
"When three bells ring, they say, 'Here is Tonda.'
When two bells ring, they say, 'Here is Tina.'
When one bell rings, it says, 'Here is Clarissa.'"
Then Lucinda does something that no one
has ever done before.
She shakes her head both back and forth,
then curls atop the earthy straw.

Professore Venuti places Clarissa in
Lucinda's arms.
She hugs the ball of
wool…but rips off its bell.
The lamb, like a heartbeat, shivers,
then licks Lucinda's cheeks.
Professore Venuti laughs. "Clarissa loves you!
Will you feed her each time
the school bell rings?"
Lucinda does not reply.

Alone one day when the lunch bell rings
and all children run for home,
Lucinda sneaks into the stalls to kneel beside
Clarissa, the lamb without a bell.
The two speak with their eyes and become friends.
For many days Lucinda feeds Clarissa,

until one day when the clouds eat the sun
and the wind swallows the valley of Santa Lucia.
The village sleeps its noonday sleep.
The cows doze beneath their olive trees.
Suddenly a flame leaps from a candle
in the lambs' stall.

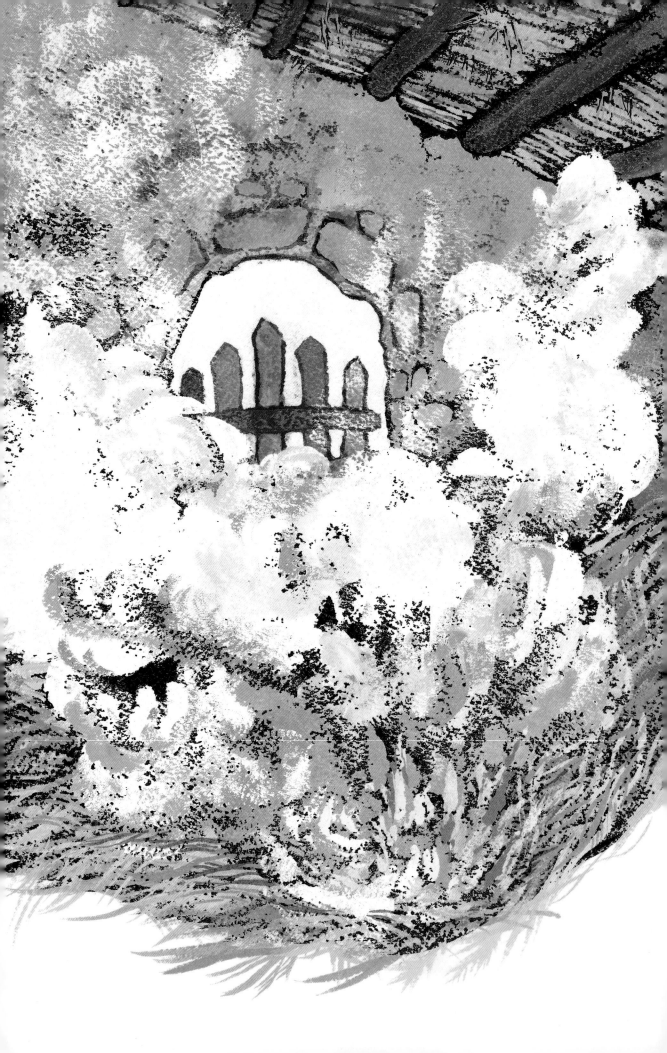

FIRE!

The dry straw burns. The old wood smokes.

Lucinda yells.

But Professore Venuti sleeps. The village sleeps.

Soon smoke fills the musty stall.

Lucinda sees nothing.

Not Tonda. Not Tina. Not Clarissa.

Lucinda yells but no one answers, except…

the bells.
Three tinkle bells whisper in the smoke.
"Here is Tonda! Help him!"
Lucinda leads Tonda to safety.
Then two bells whisper in the flames.

"Here is Tina! Help her!"
Lucinda leads Tina to safety.
She listens for Clarissa.
But the one tinkle bell does not speak.
Lucinda had never put it on again.

Lucinda runs to the Grandmother Bell
in the village square.
She stands before the large rope
that hangs from the bell tower.
But it is out of reach.
She pushes a chair beneath the rope.

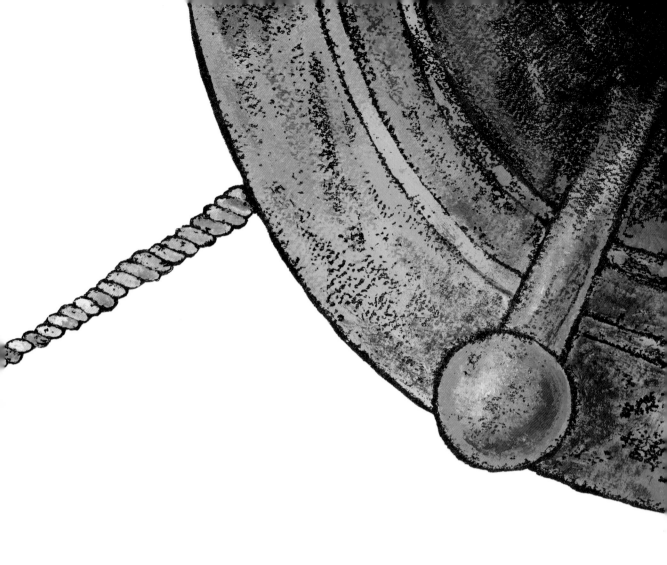

She jumps
and grabs the rope.
The rope goes down and Lucinda goes down.
The rope goes up and Lucinda goes up.
The big Grandmother Bell goes BONG! BONG!
Lucinda rises and falls with the bell.
She tightly shuts her eyes.
Her hands nearly slip from the rope.

"Hold on!" the big
Grandmother Bell cries.
"Hold on, Lucinda!"
Her hands hurt.

"I must hold on!
I WILL hold on!" she yells.
Her heart pounds;
her fingers grow weak until…

two strong hands reach up to her,
and Professore Venuti helps her down.
"You saved Clarissa and the school," he shouts.
"We heard the bell!"
Professore Venuti places the lamb
in Lucinda's arms.
"Now Clarissa belongs to you," he chuckles.
Lucinda hugs and kisses the lamb—
whose wool smells of smoke,
whose small body shakes.
Lucinda ties the small jingle bell around its neck.
"The bells spoke to you today." Mamma beams.
Lucinda smiles. "And Nonna Rosa spoke to me."

Then, as quick as the tinkle of a tiny mouse bell,
she runs out into the sun
with the lamb close behind,
to play laughing games with her friends.
From that day on, Lucinda takes good care of
Clarissa and her babies and her babies' babies.
And whenever she can,
she rings the bell of Santa Lucia
for all the world to hear.